The
Double Knights

MORE TALES

FROM

ROUND

THE

WORLD

By
JAMES McNEILL

Illustrated by
THEO DIMSON

HENRY Z. WALCK INCORPORATED   NEW YORK   1964

The
Double Knights

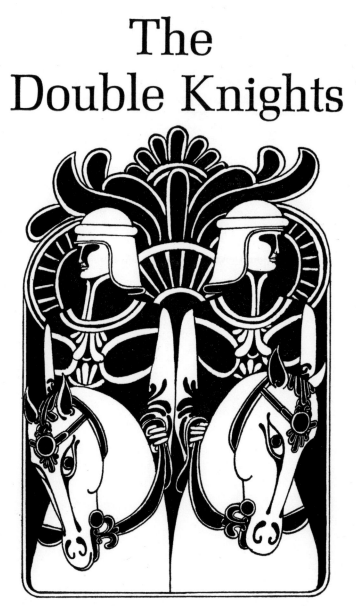

MORE TALES FROM ROUND THE WORLD

To a very brave boy named Joey

© Oxford University Press (Canadian Branch) 1964

Printed in Canada by
THE T. H. BEST PRINTING COMPANY LIMITED

CONTENTS

THE DOUBLE KNIGHTS

SPAIN

ONCE, near Barcelona in Spain, there lived an old farmer whose ancestral lands had been eaten away by poverty and debt, until nothing remained but a patch of ground with two barren olive trees, and a lowly hut.

"I think I shall become a fisherman," said the farmer to his wife one day. "If people are too poor to buy our fish, we can at least eat them ourselves."

The very first fish he caught was a fine one indeed. But scarcely had it been lifted from the net than it began to speak.

"Cut me up into eight pieces," ordered the fish. "Give the first two pieces to your wife to eat. Give two pieces to your mare and two to your dog. Then bury one piece under each of the old olive trees behind your hut."

The old man did as he was bid. Within a year his wife gave birth to twin sons, and the greatest wish of her heart came true, for she had always longed for children. She named the boys Raul and Ramon, and they were as strong and handsome as any in all of Spain.

Within the same year the mare gave birth to two fine foals, and the dog barked joyfully as she played with her two furry white puppies with black spots. As for the tired old olive trees, new green shoots burst forth in the spring so that the farmer had to hire help to gather and crush into oil the bountiful harvest.

The years flew by and Raul and Ramon grew with amazing speed. The foals became chargers such as any knight would envy, while the pups grew long and cunning.

One fine spring day the old man found hanging from each olive tree a sword of fine Toledo steel, its haft set in gold and jewels. Below each sword hung a shield emblazoned with the figure of a fish on a white field above two blue lines for the sea. As the farmer gazed the rustling leaves whispered gently, "Your sons have pure hearts, and with these weapons they will right many wrongs in the land."

Taking the swords and shields from the branches, the old man presented them to Raul and Ramon. With pride and sadness he gave each son his blessing. Then the boys, their old mother's tears on their cheeks, set off. Through Catalonia, Aragon, and Valencia they travelled, killing the wild animals that plagued the farmers and routing the bands of robbers and thieves that terrorized the countryside. In every village plaza they were hailed as heroes. People called them the Double Knights because they were as matched as two shoes, their horses as alike as two stars, and the hounds that ran ahead of them as identical as a pair of dice.

At last there came a day when the brothers decided to go separate ways. They clasped hands at a cross-road, each vowing to come to the aid of the other even if he should be at the end of the world; then Raul set off for Madrid and Ramon for Granada.

Raul found Madrid a city of sad, long-faced people instead of the gay and happy place he had heard about. "What is the matter?" he asked a weeping innkeeper.

"Each year a maiden is sacrificed to the terrible dragon," the innkeeper replied. "If this is not done, the dragon will ravage all the fields with his fiery breath and dry up all the wells by dipping his burning tail into them. The maiden's name is drawn by lot and this year the victim is the Infanta, the King's eldest daughter, and the most beautiful girl in the land. Other maidens have offered to take her place, but she will not let them, though it was her younger sister who was chosen last year."

"Why does not someone slay the beast and end this terror?" asked Raul.

"The dragon is the special pet of the King of the Moors," answered the innkeeper, wiping his eyes with his apron, "and there is not a knight in all Spain who has the courage to kill it. Already our beloved Infanta Isabella is tied to an oak tree outside the city." And the innkeeper began to weep again.

Raul rode like the wind to the Infanta. Despite her protests he cut her bonds and, lifting her upon his horse, raced to the Royal Palace. The King was overjoyed to see his daughter, though he was frightened of the dragon's revenge.

Raul did not waste a moment. Back he rode, carrying with him a mirror which he leaned against the trunk of the tree. Then he climbed up onto a branch, sword in hand, and waited for the dragon.

Soon the air was filled with a suffocating, maloderous smell of sulphur and burning grass. Then the monster came into view. Its long glowing tail wagged from side to side, its hideous claws pawed the ground as it lumbered slowly up to the oak.

When the dragon glimpsed its reflection in the mirror, it

flew into a terrible rage, thinking that another dragon had taken its place. It heaved up and fell with its whole weight against the mirror, which smashed into a thousand pieces. The beast's head hit the tree, and it lay stunned. Raul leapt from his hiding-place and ran his sword through the dragon's evil heart. The glowing tail burst into flame and consumed the rest of the slimy body.

The people of Madrid held a week-long *fiesta* to celebrate the death of the dragon. The mayor gave Raul a beautiful diamond on a golden chain to wear about his neck. But the knight had to wear it under his doublet so that he would not blind people; for, when worn by a brave man of pure heart, this diamond shone like the sun.

The Infanta Isabella and Raul, who had fallen in love, spent many happy hours together. Soon the city was celebrating the wedding of their beloved Infanta and of the knight who had rescued her. The King gave the couple a beautiful palace, and Raul and his bride lived there happily for many months.

As for the King of the Moors, he flew into a rage when told of the dragon's death, and sent out his soldiers in search of the bold knight with the curious shield who had slain his pet. The soldiers, coming upon Ramon, mistook him for his brother and captured him.

In Madrid a strange, unhappy feeling came over Raul which even his wife's love and attention could not dispel. "I must find my brother Ramon," he said to her. "I feel in my heart that he needs me."

Raul set off. For many weary months he travelled, until

at last, in the vicinity of Cadiz, he came upon an Iron Castle.

Now this castle was owned by the King of the Moors, and here Ramon was held prisoner, under the care of a grizzled witch. Once a day a small amount of food was passed to him, but not a word was spoken. His only companions were bats and spiders, but he could hear the screaming and banging of other prisoners and the raspy squeaks of the old witch as she ran from cell to cell tormenting her victims.

As soon as Raul saw the castle he felt that his brother was near. He dismounted and sounded his hunting horn before the gate. The old witch, rubbing her warty hands and smiling toothlessly, came hobbling out. For a moment she flew into a panic—the youth at the gate was so much like one of her prisoners that she thought he had escaped.

"I seek news of my brother, old woman, and my heart tells me he is here," said Raul in a firm voice.

"I live alone," the witch croaked. But seeing that he did not believe her, she added craftily, "Come in and see for yourself." And she drew a large rusty key from her pocket and unlocked the gate.

As the gate swung shut Raul left his gauntlet caught in it so that the lock did not fasten completely. The witch opened the door of the castle with another rusty key and beckoned Raul to enter. The darkness of the place rushed out at him; even the witch seemed to have disappeared, but her voice called to him, echoing back and forth from the iron walls, "Follow me, *me, me!*"

Suddenly the old witch grasped Raul's arm with her bony fingers. "Come," she cried, "we shall search downstairs."

And the walls answered back *stairs, stairs, stairs*!

The witch planned to lock Raul in the cell with his brother, but as she paused to put the key in the lock, the knight pulled the diamond from under his doublet. In the inky darkness the flame of it blinded the old woman. She rubbed her burned eyes and howled until the dungeon echoed as though a thousand lions were roaring. Her rage increased until she exploded. All that was left of her was a black cloak that wheeled through the air like a bat.

Raul quickly freed Ramon and all the other wretched prisoners. Many of them were maidens who had been sacrificed to the dragon in years past, and among them was the younger sister of the Infanta. By the light of the diamond they climbed the stairs one after another, and when all were safely through the gates, the brothers opened the windows of the Iron Castle and let the blackness out.

Raul and Ramon rode to Madrid at the head of a happy procession, and there was great rejoicing when they arrived. The Infanta's sister and Ramon fell in love and were married, and as long as the Double Knights lived, peace reigned throughout the land.

SEVEN IRON-SOLED SLIPPERS

PORTUGAL

ONCE there ruled in Portugal a king who was sorely troubled. His only daughter, Princess Harmony, wore out seven pairs of slippers every day. The King ordered the cobbler to make slippers with iron soles, but still they wore out.

"We must put an end to this," said the King, and he issued a proclamation offering Princess Harmony's hand to any man who could solve the mystery of the worn-out slippers.

Now it happened that a young orange-picker named Manoel who had lost an arm in the wars heard about the King's proclamation.

"The very thing for me," he thought. "Discovering how the Princess wears out her slippers won't be as difficult as picking oranges with one arm, and it will certainly be better than being a soldier."

Taking a bag of oranges for food, Manoel set out for Lisbon. As he trudged barefoot down the road in the hot, bright sunshine he came upon two men who were quarreling violently over a hat.

"Why are you fighting over a mere hat?" asked Manoel.

"This hat makes the wearer invisible," answered one of the men. "It belonged to our father who died without saying which of us was to inherit it."

"Allow me to help you," said Manoel. "I will throw an orange into the field, and whoever brings it back shall have the hat."

The brothers agreed. As they scrambled after the orange,

Manoel put the hat on his own head and said quickly,

"Hide me, hat, from mortal sight;
It pains me so when brothers fight."

and he was nowhere to be seen when the brothers came back, still quarreling.

Several days later Manoel came upon two more men fighting. This time it was over a pair of high leather boots.

"You shouldn't quarrel over such a trifle," said Manoel to the men when they stopped rolling in the dust.

"With these boots on your feet you travel faster than an eagle," answered one of the men. "They belonged to our father who died without saying which of us was to inherit them."

"Allow me to help you, then. I will throw an orange into the field, and whoever brings it back to me shall have the boots."

The brothers quickly agreed and, when the orange was thrown, ran after it. Manoel put on his magic hat, leapt into the boots and cried,

"Up boots and on your way.
Take me to the King today."

Across meadows and mountains he sped until he reached the palace gates, where he took off the magic hat and requested an audience with the King.

"Your Majesty," said Manoel, when he was ushered into the King's presence, "I should like a chance to win the hand of your daughter the Princess."

"Very well," said the King. "You will be given three days to discover what is happening to Princess Harmony's slippers. If you succeed, you shall be made a duke and wed the Princess. If you fail, you shall swing from the gallows."

That night Manoel sat down outside the door of the Princess's chamber. He was so tired after his long journey that he fell asleep at once and did not waken until the next morning. Beside him on the carpet lay seven pairs of worn-out slippers.

"No matter," thought Manoel. "I have two more nights in which to discover the Princess's secret."

The next night Manoel again sat down outside the door of the Princess's chamber. But try as he might, he could not keep his eyes open. It seemed that he had been dozing for just one second when he felt something brush by him. It was Princess Harmony, but she was not going out, she was coming in, and in her hand were seven pairs of worn-out slippers.

"Where have you been?" asked Manoel, and the Princess answered,

> "For me to know and you to guess.
> If you knew you'd tell the rest."

"I have one more chance," thought Manoel. "I will sleep all day and then I'll be able to stay awake tonight." He found a bed in the servants' quarters and slept soundly until supper-time.

When the sun had set Manoel took his place outside Princess Harmony's door and pretended to fall asleep. The palace clocks were chiming midnight when the Princess slipped by him, as softly as a perfumed breeze. Manoel put the magic hat on his head and followed her.

When the Princess reached the sea, a stately galleon rose out of the water to meet her. She leapt aboard, and before Manoel could follow, the galleon moved swiftly across the dark sea, then rose into the air.

Manoel cried,
> Up boots and over the water;
> Don't lose sight of the King's fair daughter"

and he was on the galleon which was now flying like a bird through the night.

A short while later, from the highest mast of the galleon a voice called out, "Land ho! The Isle of Brasil—dead ahead!"

The galleon dropped anchor, and Princess Harmony jumped into a longboat. Twenty pirates rowed her ashore and conducted her to a lighted pavilion that stood among the palm trees. A thunderous cheer rose from a crowd of captains, bosuns, and sailors who surrounded the pavilion. Music sounded and the Princess began to dance, slowly at first, then faster and faster until she spun like a top and her feet were as blurred as the wings of a humming-bird. She paused only to change her slippers as they wore out.

Manoel's magic boots had carried him to the pavilion where he studied the strange audience closely. Many of the sailors had broken necks or fearful wounds and all had strange hollow eyes. Some wore ankle chains, and still others were chained together. Their leader was a gnarled old man who wore a salt-stained admiral's hat and uniform with gold braid from his wrist to his elbow. Whenever he issued a command, the sailors obeyed him instantly, saying, "Aye, aye, Cap'n Jonah!"

The Captain was reading an ancient book in which were written all the secrets of magic that he used to raise dead pirates from the bottom of the sea. Each time he turned a page, the music became faster. Finally he closed the book and the music stopped.

The Princess sat down to rest and to eat of the abundant food set before her. When Captain Jonah joined her, Manoel stole the book and hid it beneath his coat. Then he slipped away and told his boots to carry him back to the palace.

When the Princess returned Manoel lay asleep before her door. She slipped by, leaving seven pairs of worn-out slippers beside him on the carpet.

At daybreak the King woke Manoel, shouting, "Your three nights are up, and a fine watch you have kept! Here are the Princess's new slippers, made only yesterday, and they are worn out as usual."

At that moment the Princess appeared. Manoel quickly pulled the book of magic from under his coat and opened the first page. Music came from nowhere. Princess Harmony began to dance, slowly at first, then faster and faster and faster. When Manoel closed the book the music stopped and the Princess took off her slippers. They were completely worn out!

"So *that* is the secret!" cried the King.

Manoel was made a duke and the Princess became his duchess. Sometimes he would open the magic book and watch his wife dance. But he never let her dance so long that she wore out her shoes. And he never told her of his magic boots and hat or how he discovered her secret.

SANTIAGO AND THE FIGHTING BULLS

MEXICO

ONCE upon a time, on a *rancho* in old Mexico, there lived a young man named Santiago. He and his father raised fighting bulls for their master who lived in Mexico City. From morning to night Santiago fed and watered the calves, and because he was a kind and gentle youth, he was always sad when the herders came to take the young animals away.

Santiago's dearest friend was Don Pedro, a beautiful white pony that he had raised. The pony was very wise, and often, when the two were alone, they spoke to each other. Always they talked of having a *rancho* of their own, and each week Santiago saved the few *centavos* that he earned.

One day news reached the *rancho* that four fierce bulls had escaped and were the terror of the capital. The Governor himself was offering the hand of one of his daughters and a dowry of three thousand silver *pesos* to anyone who could capture the bulls and return them to the bull ring.

"Don Pedro and I shall round up the bulls for the Governor," Santiago told his father.

"It will not be as easy as that," said his father kindly. "Those bulls are not like the calves with wobbly knees that you feed every day. They are much older, and the cruelty of humans has made them mean and angry."

Nevertheless Santiago insisted on going, and knelt down for his father's blessing.

"Be careful, my son. On the way to the capital you will pass the devil's estate. Beware, for he kills all who enter."

They travelled southward, the wise Don Pedro taking the

easiest and shortest roads. After several days they came upon a fine *hacienda*. Before it stood a handsome, courtly gentleman who invited Santiago to enter and refresh himself.

"Thank you, *Señor*," said the youth, who was very tired and hungry. "Does your kindness extend to my horse?"

"Take him to the stable. There you will find all that he needs."

At the stable Don Pedro turned to his master and began to speak. "That handsome *señor* is the devil," the horse said. "Do not eat his supper; instead slip the food inside your shirt. Then return to me and I will tell you more."

"You are a clever horse, *amigo*. I shall do as you say."

Hungry though Santiago was, he only pretended to eat the wonderful food set before him, and when the meal was done he excused himself, saying, "I must brush my horse and water him again. Then I will return."

At the watering trough Don Pedro carefully explained what his master should do. "The devil will ask you to sit up with him. Put some of my tears in your eyes to keep you awake or he will kill you. As soon as he falls asleep, slip away, taking with you only what you find on a shelf near the door."

Santiago returned to the *hacienda* and waited until the devil was asleep and snoring. Then he took a dish full of needles and a small round mirror from the shelf by the door, and went back to Don Pedro.

Through the cool night they rode, and just as the sun was rising, they heard the thunder of hooves behind them. It was the devil on a mighty red horse. All morning the chase went on, up hill and down, over rivers and fields. Suddenly the devil cursed up a hail storm and flung it after Santiago.

"Throw the needles over your shoulder, good master!" cried Don Pedro.

Santiago obeyed and a great forest of cactus sprang up. The cactus absorbed the force of the hail storm and entangled the devil's horse in its prickly grip. But he was not long delayed. Once more he was behind them, his lasso swinging over Santiago's head.

"Throw the dish at him!" cried Don Pedro.

Santiago threw the dish and a large lake appeared, nearly drowning the devil and his horse. Then Santiago threw the mirror into the water and the lake became ice in which the devil, screaming in terror, was frozen solid.

And so Santiago continued on his way unharmed.

As Mexico City came into sight, Don Pedro said, "I have heard that there is a spring nearby that has magic powers. The old drink from it and become young; the young drink from it and become old. For the work that lies ahead of us I think we should become old."

They found the enchanted spring and drank deeply of the clear water. Don Pedro became a shambling old nag with his bones sticking out. Santiago became wrinkled and scarred, with a patch over one eye. They had changed so much that they rolled on the grass laughing at each other.

"Where are the fierce wild bulls to be found?" Santiago asked a soldier, when they entered the city.

"In the municipal park, *Señor*, where they are eating the

grass and flowers. The greatest *vaqueros* in Mexico have not been able to herd them to the arena."

Santiago rode to the park. There stood four of the largest bulls he had ever seen, each bearing his master's brand. One had a twisted horn.

"Manuelito, you are a bad bull!" Santiago called. The animal with the twisted horn looked up in amazement. Then all the bulls recognized Santiago and rushed toward him, not in anger but in joy, for he was the only one who had ever been kind to them.

The crowds on the sidewalks watched in terror and wonder, and then burst into cheers as the ancient *vaquero* on his decrepit white nag herded the bulls through the streets. The Governor was overjoyed and invited Santiago to be his guest of honour at a great *corrida* the next day.

A vast crowd filled the arena. Flags were flying and the bands were playing gay music. The Governor and his six lovely daughters sat in the royal box but Santiago was not with them.

Into the bull ring came all the city dignitaries. They were followed by the four most famous *matadors* in all of Mexico. Behind the *matadors* marched the *banderilleros*. After the *banderilleros* came the *picadores* and the *chulos*.

The attendants, excited by the noise, released the four bulls from their pens all at once. Bellowing and snorting, the animals ran this way and that, tossing the *matadors* in all directions. Everyone tried to climb out of the ring at the same time.

When only the bulls remained, pawing the sand and snorting in anger, a weary old man walked into the bull-ring. He carried neither cape nor sword; instead of gay silks, he wore a weatherstained *poncho*, and his *sombrero* covered his ears.

"Ho, my brave ones!" Santiago called. "Go back to the pens, all of you, and I promise you a *rancho* where you can live in peace and be fathers to many bulls."

When the bulls had been penned, the mightiest *viva* ever heard in Mexico burst from the throats of the crowd. Some people threw flowers at the old man as he stood before the Governor.

"Excellency," begged Santiago, "instead of the reward that was promised, may I have the lives of the brave bulls? With such as these I can start my own *rancho*."

"Your wish is granted," said the Governor. "And you shall also have the reward—three thousand *pesos* and one of my daughters as your bride."

During the great *fiesta* that was held in Santiago's honour, he chose the Governor's youngest daughter to be his wife. Then, with the cheers of the happy people ringing in his ears, he left the city.

Santiago's bride was very sad. "Why could he not have been young and handsome, as well as brave," she thought. She bit her lip to keep back the tears. And when they came to the enchanted spring, she threw herself on the grass and wept while Santiago and Don Pedro drank deep of the cool water.

Imagine her surprise when Santiago gently lifted her to her feet and she found her husband was the most handsome *vaquero* in all the land!

BROTHER ANANSI AND SIR PEACOCK

TRINIDAD

ONCE upon a time, on the sunny island of Trinidad, there lived a king whose only son was mute. All the sunshine of the island could not make up for the sadness in the King's heart because the little prince could not, or would not, say a word.

Now there lived on the same island a clever rogue named Brother Anansi who was a mischievous schemer, a boaster, and a glutton. It was said that he could never do good without doing some harm; it was also said that he could never do harm without doing some good.

One day Brother Anansi decided that his talents would be useful to the King, so he went to the palace.

"I can make the young prince talk, Your Majesty," said Brother Anansi, bowing very low so the King couldn't see that he was not as confident as he sounded. "The secret is to find a voice that he likes. That will take some time, of course, and—"

"And you will want a reward," the King finished. "Very well, if you can do what you say I will give you one room filled with food, and another filled with gold and fine clothes."

Brother Anansi left the palace with mixed feelings. He had made his boast and been promised an enticing reward, but he had no idea how to accomplish his task.

On the road he met a pig. "Ho there, Brother Pig! If I were to take you to the palace to talk to the Prince, what would you say?"

"*Grunt, grunt, snuffle!*" answered the pig.

"That is no voice for a prince," said Brother Anansi, "but thank you just the same."

Further on he met a bearded goat contentedly eating nettles. "What would you say to the Prince if I could arrange to have you presented at court, Professor Goat?"

"*Beh, beh, beh!*" bleated the goat.

"That will never do," said Brother Anansi, shaking his head. "A prince couldn't have a voice like that!"

In a yard he met an old red hen with a brood of chickens. "Ho, Mother Hen!" he called. "What would you say to the Prince if I could have you presented at court?"

"*Cluck, cluck, cluck, pluck, pluck, cluck!*" said the hen.

"That is not the proper voice for a prince," thought Brother Anansi sadly, and he walked on. He was just beginning to feel discouraged when he met an ugly grey peacock in a cornfield.

"What would *you* say at court, Sir Peacock, if I could have you presented to the Prince?"

"I would say nothing at all," answered the peacock. "I am not expected to talk, but to sing. It is a well-known fact that my voice is the most beautiful in the world." There was a hint of vanity in his reply, and without further ado he jumped up on a fence, preened himself, and began to sing.

His voice was so beautiful that the breeze in the cornfield stopped to listen. The bees ceased buzzing and the leaves trembled on the branches. When the peacock finished, Brother Anansi was laughing and crying at the same time. He laughed because the peacock was so ugly and vain and

he cried because the singing and the song had touched him deeply. Here was a voice that would make the King's son speak.

"I will have to trick Sir Peacock," thought Brother Anansi, who knew that the bird was so proud of his voice that he would never part with it.

Off went Brother Anansi and persuaded the King to hold a contest at the royal palace. A great reward and a gold medal would be offered to the best singer on the island.

Two weeks passed and the great day came. The King was there, and so was the Queen, and so were all the courtiers, and the ambassadors, and the court calypso singers, and the steel drum players. Only the little dumb prince was nowhere to be seen; Brother Anansi had hidden him behind a curtain.

"Stay out of sight and be very quiet," he whispered to the boy. "From all the voices you will hear, pick the one you like best, and you may have it for your own."

The hen sang a solo full of irritating clucks. The goat gave renditions in a bleating tenor. Even the pig was heard from. Then all together they sang the national anthem through twice.

The peacock, who had come in late, listened scornfully to the ugly sounds that reached his ears. He knew that as a singer he was supreme, but he consented to perform only when the King beseeched him.

The peacock's song was the most beautiful one he had ever sung. It flooded the palace hall with melody. It was about the sea and the surf, about the workers in the fields, about the cries of the market-place, about children laughing and rain on the roof and birds in the trees, about love, and babies sleeping—all in one smooth outpouring of sound.

When the applause died away the little prince began to sing from behind the curtain. It was the peacock's song, word for word, line for line, with the same rich and haunting melody.

"My voice, my voice!" croaked the peacock. "You have tricked me!" And he chased Brother Anansi around the room, pecking furiously at the rogue's short brown legs.

The King was beside himself with joy. His son had a voice! "You have done a good deed for us," he told Brother Anansi happily, "and I will reward you." Then he suddenly became serious. "But you shall also be punished, for you have injured Sir Peacock. You shall have a room full of food as I promised, but Sir Peacock shall have the room filled with gold and fine clothes."

And so it was. To this day the peacock can only make ugly noises, but he is adorned in dazzling richness, and struts and preens himself because of it, as vain as ever. And ever since the little prince found his voice, the people have followed his example and have made their sunny island a land of song.

HAKU'S POWER

JAPAN

THERE once lived in Japan an old stonecutter named Haku who had worked for many years at his trade. His clothes were always covered with dust, and his hands were calloused from the tools he used. Often he wished that he were anything else but a stonecutter.

One hot afternoon Haku spent several hours measuring a big black boulder. Then he lay down to rest in the shade of a wall and fell asleep. Suddenly he heard the sound of ceremonial gongs. Looking up, he saw a long procession coming down the road towards him. There were hundreds of attendants, courtiers, and soldiers, and in the very centre, in a curtained chair carried by eight men, sat the Mikado.

Haku prostrated himself in the dust, not daring to raise his eyes lest he be struck dead for presuming to gaze upon the divine Emperor of all Japan.

"If only I were the Mikado," thought Haku, "instead of a lowly stonecutter," and he trembled at his blasphemous thought. But just then a marvellous thing happened!

Gone were Haku's dusty clothes and his sweat-stained head-cloth. Now he was dressed in rich silks and jewels. He parted the yellow curtains of the chair with beautifully manicured hands that could never belong to a stonecutter.

"How easily I have adjusted to my new position!" thought Haku. "Such a feeling of power! I need only ring this silver bell and servants will obey me instantly." And with that he rang the bell and bade the procession stop while he rested, for the chair was bumpy and the sun very hot.

"But Your Sublime Highness," cried the Imperial Chamberlain, "only this morning you ordered my execution if we did not reach Kyoto by sundown!"

The stonecutter-emperor was moved with pity for the unhappy chamberlain. "Oh yes, of course I did. Then let us move on."

The heat increased and Haku grew more uncomfortable. "The sun in the sky is more powerful than any emperor," he thought. "I would rather be the sun than the Mikado of Japan."

No sooner was the thought in his mind than there he was, high in the sky, shining down upon all the lands of the earth.

Haku now found that he was powerful indeed. Sometimes he scorched a field he had only intended to warm, and one day he shone too hard on the ocean and great clouds of steam climbed up into the sky. The dense cloud covered all the land, and the sun's rays could not get through.

"What is this?" thought Haku in alarm. "Are the clouds more powerful than the sun? If that is so, I will be a cloud."

No sooner was the thought in his mind than he became a huge black cloud lying low over the earth.

Haku's new power was not easy to control. He wasted a whole day pouring water on a barren desert, and he often dropped snow where he had intended to drop rain.

"What strange weather we are having this year!" said the farmers in the rice paddies. "Strange indeed!" said the women in the wheat fields.

One day Haku found himself directly over the large black

boulder on which he had been working when the Mikado passed by. "Oho!" he cried. "We'll see how long you can withstand me now!" He sent down rain in big drops and then in streams. He washed away the land and the trees and the straw-roofed houses. He rained and rained upon the black boulder but he could not move it or alter it in any way.

"Only a stonecutter can change that rock. Only a stone-cutter with good tools and great skill can make it useful or beautiful. Gladly would I be a stonecutter again!"

No sooner was the thought in his mind than he found himself lying once more in the shade of the wall. "I have slept much too long!" he cried, leaping up. And he sang as he worked—the happiest stonecutter in all Japan.

THE SEVEN SIMEONS SIMEONOVICH

RUSSIA

MANY hundreds of years ago there lived in Russia an old peasant, named Simeon, and his wife. Simeon was unhappy because he had no son to bear his name, and every night he prayed for one. When at last his prayers were answered, his wife had not one son but seven! All of them were named Simeon after their father. But alas, while they were still very young their parents died and the seven boys were left alone on the tiny farm.

One day, as they were working in the field, the Czar came riding by, accompanied by his courtiers. Seeing the seven boys, he stopped to talk to them.

"What is your name?" he asked the first lad.

"Simeon Simeonovich, your Imperial Highness."

"And your name?" he asked the second.

"Simeon Simeonovich, your Imperial Highness."

"And your name?" he asked the third.

"Simeon Simeonovich, your Imperial Highness."

"And the rest of you? I suppose you are called Simeon Simeonovich too?"

"Simeon Simeonovich we are, your Imperial Highness," the remaining four admitted. A courtier was just going to cut off their ears for their impudence when the Czar stopped him. Then one of the boys spoke again. "We were all born on the same day," he said, "and we were all named after our father."

"Come with me to my palace," said the Czar, "and I shall make you useful in the world."

At the palace a conference was held. After much discussion the boys were asked what trade or art would satisfy them most.

"If it please Your Imperial Majesty," the first Simeon said, "I will build you an iron tower that will reach to the heavens."

"So it shall be," said the ruler happily. "You may begin at once in the imperial blacksmith shop."

"Your Imperial Majesty," said the second Simeon, "when my brother has built the tower I will stand at the top of it and let you know what is happening in all the neighbouring countries."

"That will be more useful than a hundred spies," cried the Czar gleefully. "So be it."

"If my brother will forge an axe for me," said the third Simeon, "I will cut trees in the imperial forest and fashion them into ships for you."

Then the fourth Simeon said, "When my brother has built a ship, I will command it. If we are in danger of capture by an enemy, I will grasp my vessel by the prow and pull it down to the undersea kingdom. When the enemy thinks we have been sunk, we will rise from the water and take them by surprise."

"And you?" asked the Czar of the fifth Simeon. "What would it please you to do in my service?"

"Your Imperial Majesty," answered the lad, "have my brother fashion a gun for me in the imperial shop. With this gun I will be able to shoot any bird that flies."

Then the sixth Simeon said to the monarch, "I am a fast

runner, and will retrieve any bird my brother shoots before it can touch the ground."

"And what is *your* wish?" the Czar asked the seventh and last Simeon.

"I need neither art nor craft," the lad replied, "for already I have a valuable skill. I am a thief."

"A thief!" exclaimed the Czar. "In my realm thieves are hanged."

"Wait!" cried the chief courtier. "If he is a clever thief, he may prove useful to you."

"How could a mighty Czar such as I have use for a common thief?"

The courtier smiled slyly. "For many years now," he said, "Your Imperial Highness has sought the hand of the fair Princess Holena, but in vain. If this boy is so clever, he could steal the Princess for you."

The Czar turned to the lad and asked, "Can you travel over nine and twenty kingdoms and, in the thirtieth, steal the beautiful Princess Holena for me?"

"You have only to command," replied the thief.

"I command it, then. Choose what men and treasure you need and set off at once."

"I need only my brothers to help me," was the answer.

The first Simeon began working on his tower. When it was halfway to the sky the second Simeon climbed up until he could see the castle where the fair Holena lived. He called down to the Czar, "Your Imperial Majesty, beyond nine and twenty countries there sits at the window of a palace a beautiful princess."

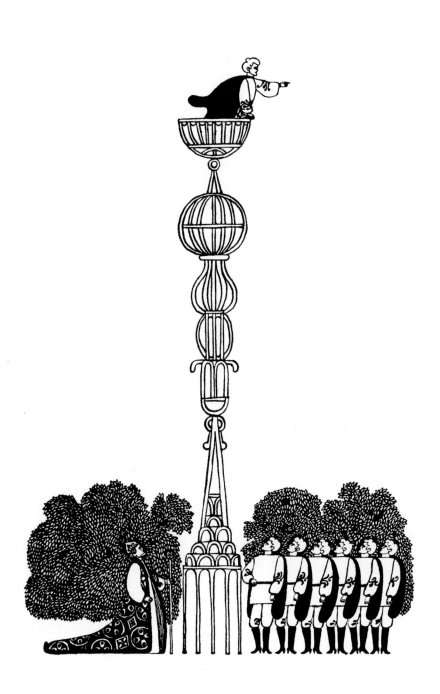

"Hurry, Simeons Simeonovich! Bring her to me," begged the Czar, "for I cannot live without her!"

The first Simeon made an axe for the third Simeon, and a gun for the fifth Simeon, while the Simeon who was a thief made friends with a stray yellow cat in the courtyard. The cat was very wise, and when the brothers set out on their journey he went with them, running ahead to find the easiest path.

When they came to the ocean, the third Simeon found a large oak tree growing close to the shore, and with his axe he chopped and chopped until the oak fell with a mighty crash into the water. In a few moments he fashioned it into a ship which the brothers filled with many precious gifts the Czar had given them. The fourth Simeon sailed the ship across the ocean to the land where the Princess Holena lived. There he cast anchor.

In the morning the thief and his cat went for a walk together. Now in this land cats were unknown. As the thief passed the royal palace the Princess spied him and his strange pet, and sent a servant running after them.

"Our mistress the Princess wishes to know what kind of dog that is," the servant said when he had overtaken the thief.

At the mention of the word "dog" the cat leapt up on his master's shoulder, meowing very loudly, and frightening the servant.

"Do not be afraid," said the seventh Simeon. "Tell your mistress that he is called a 'cat' and is really a very gentle and loyal pet."

"Wait here," cried the servant, and he ran back to tell the
Princess what he had learned. In a few moments he returned
carrying a large bag.

"My mistress wishes to buy the cat from you," he said,
proffering the open bag to the thief, who saw that it was full
of gold.

"Tell her that I will not sell the cat; but if he pleases her
she would honour me greatly by accepting him as a present
from a humble sailor."

The seventh Simeon was led to the Princess who took the
purring cat in her arms and invited the thief to go with her
to see her father.

The King was greatly pleased with the animal. "Stay a
while at my palace," he said. "It will give the cat a chance
to get used to his new home."

"I can come to the palace every day, if it please Your
Majesty, but my ship is in the harbour and I must keep close
by it at night."

Every morning for seven days the seventh Simeon
appeared at the palace and spent many hours with the
Princess and the cat. On the morning of the eighth day he
asked her if she would bring the cat and visit him.

"I should like to show you the marvelous ship I have,
made entirely from the wood of one oak tree. We have a
cargo of rare goods on board, the like of which has not been
seen in thirty lands."

The King gave his permission, but ordered the Princess to
take all her attendants with her.

When they reached the ship, the thief whispered to the

Princess, "None but you may look upon the surprise that is hidden below. Tell your servants to wait for you on deck."

Princess Holena did as the thief bade her and then followed him deep into the hold of the ship where she saw things whose beauty made her lose track of time completely.

Meanwhile the brothers weighed anchor and set sail. The ship was far out at sea when the Princess returned to the deck.

"You have tricked me!" she cried. Instantly she chanted a magic rhyme, changed into a graceful white swan, and flew away towards her home.

The fifth Simeon seized his gun and shot her.

The sixth Simeon caught her before she struck the water and carried her back to the ship where she turned from a swan into a princess.

Meanwhile the King had sent his fleet in pursuit of the Princess. As it approached the Simeons' ship, the fourth Simeon seized his oaken vessel by the prow and dragged it down to the undersea kingdom. Thinking Princess Holena had drowned, the fleet gave up the search and returned to the King with the sad news.

When darkness fell, the oaken ship surfaced and sailed on.

After many months of adventure the seven brothers reached their own country. As soon as Princess Holena met the Czar she fell in love with him and they were married at once.

As for the seven Simeons, the happy Czar made them all dukes, and for the rest of their days they lived with riches and honour.

THE FARMER'S CLEVER DAUGHTER

ESTONIA

ONCE upon a time there was a clever though conceited king who ruled Estonia. He wanted to marry, but alas, try as he might, he could not find a bride quite as clever as himself. The daughters of other kings were charming but dull. The daughters of nobles were incapable of clever conversation. The daughters of generals and merchants could only talk of money, and the daughters of peasants and farmers were far beneath a king.

Now it chanced that one day an old grey plough horse strayed into the King's hayfield and was seized. This horse belonged to a poor farmer who went to the King and begged on his knees to have the animal returned to him.

"Without my mare to plough the land," he said, "my wife, my son and my two daughters would starve."

"If you can answer two questions you may have the horse," said the King. "If not, it shall be mine."

"Very well," replied the farmer, certain that he would not get his horse back from the crafty ruler.

The first question the King asked was, "How far away is heaven?" And the second question was, "How big is the moon?"

The farmer begged the King for a day to think of the answers. That evening he asked his eldest daughter, who was both clever and witty.

The next day he returned to the palace and faced the King.

"The answer to your first question, Your Majesty, is one day's journey."

"How is that?" asked the King. "Have you been there?"

"No, Your Majesty," replied the farmer, "but remember, our Lord said to the thief on the cross, 'This day thou shalt be with me in paradise.' So it must be but one day's journey. The answer to the second question is the size of a penny, because as anyone can see, a penny held before the eye just hides the moon."

The King returned the horse as he had promised, but he was puzzled and curious to know how a simple farmer could answer such difficult riddles. The very next day, disguised as a peddlar, he went to the farmer's house, and was met at the door by the farmer's elder daughter.

"Where is your father?" asked the King.

"He went out to make better out of good," she replied.

"Where is your mother?"

"She is with the black dog in the birch grove. What she catches she throws away, and what she does not catch she brings home," said the maid.

"Where is your sister?" asked the King, amazed at the replies.

"She is in the field turning her back to the wind."

"Where is your brother?"

"He is not in heaven or on earth."

"You have answered with clever riddles," cried the King, "but for the life of me I cannot guess their meanings!"

"My father is at the mill," said the girl simply, "grinding the grain, which is good, into flour, which is better. My mother is picking fleas from the fur of our big black dog; those she does not catch come home again. You can see my

sister in the field burning leaves; she is turning her back to the wind because of the smoke."

"All this is true," admitted the King, "but what of your brother who is not in heaven or on earth?"

"There he is, up in the pear tree picking the fruit," replied the girl.

"Very clever riddles indeed," said the King. Then he told her who he was and invited her to come and see him at the palace the next afternoon.

"But," he said, "you must not come dressed or undressed, not on foot or in a carriage or on horseback. You must not come by road or by footpath. And you must not come into the palace or remain outside."

"Very well, Your Majesty," said the girl with a curtsy.

The next day she wrapped herself in a fishnet and tied the net around the neck of a nanny goat, in such a way that she could unfasten it easily. She was quite comfortable as the goat walked aimlessly across the fields, nibbling the green grass. When the goat saw the fine green lawns of the palace it went to them and the girl guided it to the palace door. She unfastened herself from the goat's neck and, holding the net tightly about her, set one foot carefully inside the palace door so that she was neither in nor out. Then she called loudly for the King.

"For many years I have been seeking a queen as clever as myself," said the King happily when he saw the farmer's daughter. "Now I have found one. If you promise not to meddle in my affairs, I will make you my bride."

In a short time they were married and the girl was

crowned queen of the land. Everyone admired her wisdom and beauty, but no-one knew that she was only the daughter of a poor farmer. The King took great delight in his wife's clever company and they were very happy.

A few years later the King was riding one day on his handsome charger, and passed the field where the Queen's father was ploughing. A small colt followed the mare up and down the field. When it spied the King's beautiful steed, it whinnied joyfully and set off in pursuit, following the handsome horse to the royal stables.

Greatly distressed, the farmer went to the King and begged for the return of the colt, but the King said, "If this were indeed your colt it would have stayed with your mare. It must belong to my stallion and I intend to keep it."

The farmer departed sadly. On the way out of the palace he met the Queen. She listened to her father's tale of woe, whispered something in his ear, and hurried on.

The next day the King spied the farmer in the courtyard, sifting sand through his fingers.

"What are you doing?" he asked.

"I am fishing, Your Majesty."

"Fishing!" shouted the King, and he roared with laughter. "Whoever heard of catching fish in a sand pile?"

"It is as possible for fish to live in a sand pile as it is for a stallion to have a colt," replied the farmer.

The King admitted that he had been beaten at his own game and he returned the colt to the farmer. But he knew that the farmer had not wits enough to think up such a clever scheme; only the Queen could have devised it. That night the King told her that she must leave the palace forever.

"You have broken our agreement," he said. "You promised never to meddle in my affairs. But there will be no need for you to live in poverty. You may take with you whatever in the palace is most precious to you."

"I will leave tomorrow," said the Queen quietly.

That evening the Queen cooked a fine meal with her own hands and she and her husband ate and talked together. The King was close to changing his mind about sending his wife away when he suddenly fell asleep, for the Queen had put a potion in his wine. At once she bade the servants lift him into a cart and take him to her old home.

"Where am I?" cried the King when he woke to find himself lying on a cot in a smoky little cottage.

"Dear husband," the Queen said calmly, "you promised that I could take from the palace whatever was most precious to me. I have taken you because you are the dearest thing in the world."

The King was overcome with emotion, and begged her forgiveness. Together they returned to the palace, and never again did the clever Queen need to outwit the clever King.

THE THREE SUITORS

INDIA

MANY generations ago in the ancient Indian province of Bengal there lived a famous Governor who was content with his lot in life, for he had a charming wife, and a brilliant son to follow in his footsteps. Indeed, his only worry was his daughter Soma. According to the custom of the land, her family must choose a husband for her, but she was not an easy girl to please.

"I shall marry only a magician," Soma told her father. "He must be a very clever magician who can create everything my heart desires."

Because he loved his daughter very much, the Governor promised that he would do all he could to find such a man.

"I can marry only a great hero," Soma told her brother. "He must be so brave that he can protect me from any danger, and so famous that all the other women will envy me."

Because he loved Soma very dearly, her brother made a vow that he would not rest until he found such a man.

"I can marry only a wise man," Soma told her mother. "He must be able to see into the future, into the far corners of the world and into the depths of the human heart."

And the good woman promised to pray without ceasing that she might find such a man.

Now it happened that the Governor had to pay a state visit to the Sultan of Delhi. As he was preparing for his journey, he was approached by a young magician who was anxious to marry his daughter.

"Show me something of your magic powers," said the Governor, "but be quick about it, for I have a long journey before me."

"I can shorten all journeys," the Magician answered, and with a wave of his hand he changed the Governor's palanquin into a shining gold coach with wings. He opened the door, helped the Governor aboard, and then mounted the coachman's seat. In a twinkling the carriage was high in the air and flying swiftly westward over the rivers and fields of India. A few moments later it landed on the lawn of the Sultan's palace.

"A marvel!" cried the Governor in delight. "Come to my house on the first of next month and you shall marry my daughter."

At about the same time a renowned hero approached Soma's brother and begged him for his sister's hand.

"There is no enemy that I cannot defeat," the Hero said. "I fight for right and justice, for love and honour. My sword has routed whole regiments of our country's enemies."

To prove the truth of his statement, he fought the Governor's entire bodyguard then and there. His sword spun with the speed of a hummingbird's wings, until the guards were put to flight.

"You are indeed the very man to win my sister's heart," the happy brother said. "Come to our house on the first day of next month and the wedding will take place."

That very same day, as Soma's mother was in the marketplace, she was approached by a young man with sad eyes who wore a long white robe covered with mystic signs. He greeted her with careful courtesy and said, "I am a seer and a prophet, and I know that you are searching for one such as I to marry your only daughter."

"How could you know?" asked the mother in astonishment. "I have told no one of it."

"I read the hearts of people like a scroll set before my eyes," replied the Wise Man quietly.

"That you have proved without a doubt," said the mother. "Come to our house on the first day of next month and the wedding shall take place."

On the first day of the month, all three suitors, in their wedding clothes, went to the bride's house. When they saw each other they all began to talk at the same time, while Soma's parents and brother shouted at one another. The servants ran among them to hear as much as they could. Soon half the people in the city were gossiping about the dilemma of the suitors.

At last the desperate Governor went to fetch his daughter so that she could choose for herself. But the window of her room was wide open and Soma was nowhere to be seen.

The Governor hastened to consult the three suitors, for without a bride there could be no wedding.

After a moment's thought the Wise Man spoke. "She has been stolen away by the dragon Rasikin. His cave is many days' journey from here, beyond the Himalayas, and is impossible to reach at this season of the year."

"With my magic I will shorten the journey," cried the Magician. He mumbled an ancient rhyme, waved his arm, and lo, a war-chariot stood before them!

The three suitors climbed into it and sailed higher and higher into the sky until the giant mountains lay below them like white ant-hills. Soon the Wise Man spied the cave of Rasikin and they descended, landing close by it.

The dragon rushed at them. The Wise Man and the Magician cowered in fear, but the Hero, his sword gleaming in his hand, advanced fearlessly towards the beast. The fight that ensued was terrible to behold. It went on for three days and three nights, up and down the valleys, until at last the Hero lopped off the dragon's hideous head and Rasikin lay lifeless forever.

The three suitors and Soma mounted the magic chariot and sailed home again. Try as she might, however, Soma could not make up her mind which of the three great men to marry. In despair her father suggested that they seek the opinion of the most learned judge in all India. The suitors agreed to be bound by the judge's decision and they set off to plead their cases before him.

The judge listened carefully to all three. For a long time he was silent; then he said, "Soma must marry the Hero."

"Had it not been for me," the Wise Man objected, "we would never have found her."

"Had it not been for my magic," the Magician cried, "we could not have reached her in time to save her life."

"That is true," said the judge, "but the Hero won her with his brave heart. You two, like his sword, were merely instruments."

And the advice was sound, for Soma and her Hero lived a long and happy life.

THE JUDGEMENT OF HAILU

ETHIOPIA

MANY years ago, in the city of Addis Ababa, capital of the ancient country of Ethiopia, there was a rich merchant who had all that money could buy or heart could wish for. He lived in a fine house and owned many slaves.

One night, as a cold wind blew across Addis Ababa from the high plateaus, the merchant watched from his window as the beggars ran about seeking shelter in doorways.

"Arha," he said, turning to one of his slaves who was busy piling fuel on the hearth. "Arha, how much cold can a man bear? Is it possible that a man could stand naked on the top of a mountain all night and be alive in the morning?"

"I do not know, master," replied Arha. "Perhaps if a man had enough to gain, he would be able to stand the cold."

"I'll wager you could not do it, Arha."

"I have no money with which to bet, master."

"You need wager nothing," said the merchant. "If you can survive one night on the west mountain, without clothes and without a fire, I will give you your freedom and ten acres of land. If you die, I will bury you with honour."

Now Arha had always dreamed of having a little farm of his own. To make his dream come true, he was willing to risk anything. He would accept his master's challenge!

Though Arha's friends feared for his life, they admired his courage and promised to climb the mountain to the east of the city and light a fire on its peak. There would be no heat from the distant fire, but it would keep him company during the long vigil.

And so the next night Arha found himself alone on the top of the west mountain. It was bitterly cold. The icy wind chilled his bones. One by one the lights of the great city below blinked out, and the night mist folded over it.

Arha began to think he could stand the cold no longer. Suddenly on the east mountain on the other side of the city he saw the flickering light of the fire his friends had lit. He pretended that he was standing beside it, and that the warmth of it went through him. All night long he fixed his eyes on the distant glow.

At last the morning sun reddened the east, and the merchant's servants came to get Arha. He was barely able to move, but he was alive!

"You are a free man," said the merchant. "But how did you manage to stay awake and not freeze to death?"

"I would surely have died," answered Arha, "had not my friends kept a fire burning on the east mountain."

"One of my conditions was that there be no fire!" the merchant cried.

"The fire was ten miles away," protested Arha. "No warmth could come from it."

But the merchant insisted that he had won.

Arha took the matter to court. The judge, who was skilled in interpreting the letter of the law, ruled against him, saying, "It was one of your master's conditions that there should be no fire."

Then Arha heard of another judge who was so old and so wise that it was said he had studied law in the court of King Solomon himself. This judge was called Hailu, and at the first opportunity Arha went in search of him.

Hailu listened quietly to Arha's story, and when it was finished said, "Return to your master and say nothing. You will know my decision in due time."

Some days passed and Judge Hailu sent an invitation to many well-known people in Addis Ababa to come and dine with him. Among the guests were the rich merchant and the judge who was skilled in the letter of the law.

When all the guests were assembled in the great hall of Judge Hailu's house, the doors of the kitchen opened. What a mingling of delicious odours wafted out! There was the smell of bread baking, of chickens roasting, of mutton on the spit, of spices and coffee. The guests, who were very hungry, fell silent waiting for the food to be served. They waited and waited.

At last Judge Hailu rose and said, "I thank you, dear friends, for having been my guests at this feast!"

"We have had nothing to eat!" cried the merchant.

"But did you not smell the food?" asked Hailu.

"Yes, but to smell is not to eat. It does not fill the stomach."

"If your servant could be warmed by the sight of a distant fire, then you can be fed by the smell of unseen food!" was Hailu's reply.

The judge who was learned in the letter of the law recognized the truth of the words and reversed his decision. The rich merchant, ashamed of his cruelty, gave Arha cattle and horses and sheep with which to begin his new life.

And so, at last, Arha had his farm.

THE STUDENT WHO BECAME A PRINCE

HUNGARY

THERE once lived in Hungary a young man named Janos who craved knowledge and spent all his time listening to the scholars of his town. When he had learned everything they could teach him, he decided to set out for a great university in a neighbouring country.

Before he was very far on his journey, he saw a field of wild peas. Like most students, Janos was very poor, so he picked and shelled enough peas to fill his pockets. Then he continued on his way.

That night Janos came to the palace of the King of the land, and stopped at the gate to ask if he might have shelter for a night's rest. The gatekeeper took him to the chamberlain, who was very impressed by the student's wise speech and excellent grammar.

"This is no ordinary peasant," he thought, "but some rich man's son travelling in disguise to protect his wealth from robbers. No doubt his bulging pockets are filled with gold."

The chamberlain presented Janos to the Queen and the Princess. The Queen was very taken with his manners and his intelligent conversation. The Princess was also impressed —not so much with his manners and learning as with his handsome face and noble bearing. Both agreed that he must be a prince in disguise.

"It may well be that he is a prince and not a student as he claims," said the King, when his wife told him about Janos. "Invite him to dine with us and we shall see."

That evening, when Janos sat down at the table, he took only a small portion of each food, though he had never seen such sumptuous fare, and he ate very slowly because he wanted to taste each morsel to the fullest.

After the meal the King took his wife aside and said, "He certainly does not eat like a hungry student, but I am not yet convinced that this young man is a prince in disguise. I have another test in mind. Tonight we will give him a hard bed. If he is truly a prince he will not be able to sleep in such discomfort."

"An excellent idea!" exclaimed the Queen.

That night Janos was shown to a poor room in the servants' quarters. As he prepared for bed he accidentally spilled the dried peas from his pockets; they rolled over the floor and into the cracks between the boards. He spent all night picking them up, for his frugality would not allow him to lose one pea.

The next morning Janos was red-eyed from sleeplessness. But still the King was not convinced.

That night Janos was taken to the royal guest-room where the bed was wonderfully soft. He was so tired that he slept like a pumpkin.

At last the King and the Queen agreed that Janos must indeed be a prince, and they invited him to stay with them for as long as he wished. The royal tailor outfitted him with fine clothes, and everyone treated him with great respect, calling him "Your Highness", though Janos told them he was not a prince. He soon stopped protesting, however, for he was beginning to enjoy his new life.

Janos was much in demand at court because of his learning, and it was not long before he was made adviser to the
King on matters of law and state. He saw the Princess often,
and in time they fell in love and were married.

A year passed. One day the King summoned his daughter
and son-in-law. He told them he was growing old and
wanted Janos to be his heir. "Journey to your home one last
time," he commanded, "for when you become king, there
will be no opportunity to do so."

The next day Janos and the Princess and their attendants
set out. Janos was greatly distressed, for he knew that very
shortly his unwilling deception would be found out. At last
he decided that he must resume his rightful role as a student.

While the party was passing through a dense wood he
slipped away, but he had not gone very far when an old hag
approached him.

"What are you doing in my forest?" she cackled.

Janos told her all that had befallen him and how he must
now leave forever his dear wife and his new-found role as
heir to the throne.

"Go back to your wife," the old woman commanded. "On
the other side of this forest, standing high on a mountain
top, you will find a copper castle that belongs to a seven-
headed dragon. Tell your wife that it is your castle, and that
all the lands about are yours also. If the dragon should return while you are there, take as many loaves of bread as
you can and set them outside the gate, adding this loaf to
the rest," and she handed him a loaf of bread that was very
heavy and quite hard.

Janos thanked her warmly and rode off to join the rest of the party. Taking the lead, he directed them out of the forest, and there on a high mountain stood a copper castle that glistened in the sun. Below the mountain was a wide, fertile valley with farmland as far as the eye could see.

The Princess and Janos were so happy living in the castle that they stayed there for nearly a year. Then one night a terrible rumbling woke them from their sleep and Janos ran out to see what was happening. An excited servant shouted that a seven-headed dragon was coming up the mountainside. Janos quickly took all the bread from the pantry and set it outside the gate. Into the pile he slipped the loaf the old woman had given him.

The hungry dragon stopped to eat, gobbling up the loaves seven at a time with his seven mouths. But he could not eat the loaf of hard bread. He bit it so hard with his first mouth that he snapped off all his teeth; then he put it in his second mouth and the same thing happened. As soon as the dragon had broken off all the teeth in his seven mouths, Janos and his servants rushed out and put the beast to death.

The instant this was done, the strange old hag whom Janos had met in the forest appeared. "You have destroyed the terror of this valley," she said, "and you deserve a fitting reward. The copper castle and all the land around is yours forever."

The happy youth was now a true prince. When he inherited his father-in-law's kingdom, he ruled wisely, and built schools and universities. And he and his queen lived happily ever after.

CATHERINE AND THE FATES

ITALY

ONCE there lived in Italy a rich merchant who had more treasures than the King. But his chief treasure and the love of his heart was his daughter Catherine who was mistress of his house because his wife was dead. Though Catherine was young, she was skilled in many arts, and she was as gracious as she was accomplished.

One day as she was sewing in her chamber, the door opened and a tall, beautiful lady entered, holding a wheel in her hand. Catherine was so astonished she could not speak. Before she could collect herself, the tall woman said, "When would you rather enjoy your life, in youth or in old age?"

For a moment Catherine was unable to answer. "If I say 'in youth'," she thought, "I must suffer in old age."

The beautiful intruder repeated the question.

"Let me enjoy my life in old age," said Catherine. "In youth God's will be done."

The lady spun the wheel she held in her hand. "I am your Fate," she said. "As Fate has decreed, so shall it be accomplished." And she disappeared.

A few days later Catherine's father received news that a terrible storm at sea had wrecked his fleet of ships, and that all the goods and sailors were lost. Scarcely a month passed before his lands and houses were seized by his debtors and he was put in prison, leaving his daughter penniless and alone. Stricken with grief, he fell ill and died.

A few days later a Contessa chanced to see Catherine

crying in the street and said to her, "Why are you weeping, my child?"

"Ah, noble lady, I have gone for many days without food, and many nights without a bed to sleep in. Have you a place for me in your household?"

"Indeed I have," answered the Contessa. She took Catherine into her home, and was soon praising the girl's many skills.

Time passed. One day the Contessa put Catherine in charge of the house while she went visiting. "Take good care," she warned the girl before she left, "and let no one in."

Catherine bolted all the doors and fastened the windows. Then she began to sew. But as she worked, the door opened by itself and the tall woman appeared again.

"Ah Catherine, did you think that I was going to leave you in peace?" the Fate said. She ran to the linen closet, took out all the fine cloths and spreads, and ripped them into tiny pieces.

"Woe is me!" cried Catherine, wringing her hands. "I must flee the city before my mistress returns!"

No sooner had Catherine gathered her shabby belongings together and left, than the Fate restored everything to perfect order.

When the Contessa returned, she found everything immaculate. She wished to reward Catherine and to promote her in the household, but she searched for the girl in vain.

For many days Catherine walked, making her bed in the fields by the road. At last she came to a large city and found a position in the home of a Marchesa. The children loved her, and she was soon trusted with their care.

One day as the Marchesa departed for church, she told Catherine to put the children to bed for a nap and on no account to let anyone in. Catherine shut the doors tightly, tucked the children in bed, and sang a lullaby to them. When they were all asleep, the door opened and there once again stood her Fate.

"Did you think you could escape me, Catherine?" and the Fate laughed. She woke all the children and they cried in terror.

Poor Catherine was at her wit's end. "I must leave at once," she moaned, and began to pack.

No sooner was she out of the city than the Fate sang a song and the children all fell asleep again with smiles on their rosy faces. When the Marchesa returned home and found all her children sleeping so peacefully, she went to find Catherine to thank her, but the girl was nowhere to be seen.

And so it went, on and on. Whenever things were going well for Catherine, her Fate intervened and she had to start over again. Seven years passed in this way.

One morning as Catherine was walking through a little town, tired and hungry, she caught the odour of fresh-baked bread. It came from a little bakeshop, and Catherine went in and inquired whether she might earn some of the bread for herself.

"I will give you a place," said the old baker-woman, "if you will perform a task for me. Do you see the high moun-

tain yonder? Every morning you must climb it, carrying a
board covered with fresh bread. When you reach the top
you must cry out like a peddlar 'Oh my mistress's Fate!'
three times in a loud voice. Then my Fate will appear and
take the bread."

Catherine consented. She remained with the old woman
for a year, doing her task well. Every morning she got up
early and took the fresh-baked bread up the high mountain.
When she reached its summit, she called out three times
and a beautiful tall woman appeared and took the bread
from her, returning in its stead the board that Catherine
had brought the day before.

The climb was a long hard one, and Catherine was often
so tired when she got back to the bakeshop that she would
fall to weeping.

"What ails you, girl?" her mistress asked one day.

Catherine told of the decision she had once had to make
and what had befallen her since. "Surely," she said, "these
eight years I have suffered are enough sorrow for one life."

"Tomorrow when you return to the mountain, ask my
Fate to try and persuade your Fate to leave you in peace."

The next morning when Catherine reached the summit
of the mountain with the loaves, she said to the tall lady,
"Oh my mistress's Fate! I pray you, beg my Fate to perse-
cute me no longer."

"Your Fate is now asleep," answered the woman. "But I
shall give you her answer tomorrow."

After Catherine left, the baker-woman's Fate went to the
young girl's Fate and woke her. "Dear sister," she said,

"will you never weary of making poor Catherine suffer? Permit her to see some happy days again."

The sleepy Fate held out a little piece of coloured silk. "Give her this," she said, "and tell her to preserve it carefully." And the Fate went back to sleep.

When Catherine received the silk she took it to her mistress. "What can I do with this?" she asked. "It is too small even for a kerchief!"

"Keep it as you were instructed," the baker-woman replied, "for who knows what use it may some day have?"

Soon after this the town-crier called all the people together in the market-place. He told the assembled crowd that the Crown Prince was about to be married. The finest cloak in all the world had been made for him, with the rarest of silken fabrics, but alas, a small piece of silk was missing. A large reward was being offered to anyone who could bring to the palace some silk that would match the cloak so that the royal tailors could finish the garment.

Catherine set off with the silk that her Fate had given her and, of all the thousands of pieces the people brought to the court, hers was the only one whose colour and size were exactly right.

"It is worth its weight in gold!" cried the King. And his treasurer brought a delicate set of balances. Putting the silk on one side, the King carefully laid a gold coin on the other.

Now one gold coin should have been equal to the tiny piece of silk, but the scales did not move. The King piled on more and more gold coins until he had emptied the royal coffers, and still the scales did not move.

"What magic is this?" he cried in terror.

"It is no magic," answered the Crown Prince. "It is a sign that this lovely girl was meant to be my wife."

The King asked his wise men if this could be so, and they replied that there was only one test in the world that could prove it right or wrong. Taking the King's crown from his head, they laid it on top of the pile of gold and lo, the scales balanced!

The Crown Prince fell on his knees before Catherine and asked her to be his wife and to inherit the kingdom with him. All the people cheered, and from that time on, Catherine's life was filled with happiness and love.

THE PRINCESS AND THE SHEPHERD

FRANCE

Long ago in France there lived a king who had a beautiful, clever, conceited daughter. Since she was an only child, her father gave her everything her heart could wish for. When she reached the age to marry, it proved difficult to find a proper husband for her; the clever princes were too ugly and the handsome princes were too stupid.

"This is a very serious problem," said the King. "I will have to sit on my throne and think."

For ten days he sat without moving. The whole court held its breath, until at last the King called for his page to bring quills and paper.

"I will send word over all the land. Any man who can pass three tests that I have devised is fit to marry my daughter, and to rule the kingdom as well."

Court criers were sent forth, and a holiday was granted for the contest. When the appointed day arrived, more than one hundred knights and nobles, with their prancing steeds and their attendants, gathered in the courtyard.

"Climb the tower," said the King to his daughter, "and throw this golden snuffbox from the highest window. The suitor who returns it shall have first chance at the tests."

When the Princess looked down from the tower, the men below seemed like so many ants milling about. "I will throw the snuffbox far out and watch them scramble for it," she thought mischievously, and sent it flying through the air.

But the golden snuffbox fell to the ground outside the castle walls, where it was picked up by the King's shepherd.

82

He saw that the box was inscribed with the royal insignia and decided to return it.

When a servant brought in the snuffbox and reported who had found it, the Princess turned pale. "I could never marry a ragged shepherd!" she cried.

"I must let him have his chance," said the King, "for I have given my royal word. But have no fear. The tasks I have devised are too difficult for a servant to perform."

The shepherd was brought before the King, who said, "You must herd one hundred rabbits in the forest for a whole day and bring them back at night. If you fail, you will lose your head."

The next morning, deep in the woods, the royal clerk released one hundred rabbits from a large cage, and went back to the palace. The shepherd, whose name was Gaston, watched the rabbits run helter-skelter through the forest. Then he drew a battered old pipe from the pocket of his ragged jacket and began to play a tune that was very sad.

Now this was a magic pipe, and as Gaston played, all the wild animals in the woods gathered about him. At last he made a mournful little trill, and the rabbits began to appear—first one, then two, then ten, twenty, fifty, until all had returned. When the shepherd finished playing the wild animals departed, but the rabbits stayed, huddling close to the old stump on which Gaston sat.

In the meantime the Princess began to fear the outcome of Gaston's task.

"After all," she thought, "he does herd the royal sheep! Perhaps he knows how to herd rabbits as well."

She dressed as a peasant girl and went to find Gaston.

"Would you give a poor girl one of your fine rabbits for her supper?" she begged.

"I will give you a rabbit in exchange for a kiss," said Gaston slyly. The Princess gave him a dainty kiss and he put a rabbit in her basket. But before she was far away he played the mournful trill on his pipe and the rabbit leapt out of the basket and returned to him.

Late in the afternoon the King also became worried. He disguised himself as a peddlar and, riding on a donkey, came to find Gaston in the woods.

"Would you give a poor traveller one of your fine rabbits for his supper?" he begged.

"If you will kneel down and kiss your donkey three times on the nose," said Gaston, "you may have your choice of my rabbits."

Three times the King kissed the donkey on the nose and three times the donkey brayed.

But before the King was far away Gaston played the trill again, and back came the rabbit to lie panting beside him.

As the sun was setting the King's clerk appeared once more, and carefully counted the rabbits as Gaston led them into the cage. Then together they returned to the palace to tell the King that the first task had been completed.

"Your second task shall not be as easy as the first," said the King craftily. "In the granary, all in one pile, are four hundred bushels of flax, three hundred bushels of wheat, and one hundred bushels of oats. Tonight, with only a candle for light, you must separate the grain into three piles.

If, in the morning, I find one kernel of wheat in the oats or one flax-seed in the wheat you will lose your head."

That night Gaston sat down in the granary and began to play his pipe softly and slowly. First one, then two, then ten, twenty, fifty, hundreds of small black ants appeared and began to sift the grain.

When the clerk unlocked the door of the granary in the morning the King and the Princess saw that Gaston's task had been completed. The Princess, filled with admiration, began to think that perhaps Gaston would not be such a poor choice after all. But the King was furious.

"The third task will not be so easy," he said rather desperately. "Until now you have only needed patience and diligence. To rule, you must have a clever tongue as well." Then he gave Gaston a large sack and commanded him to fill it with lies to the very top. And to make sure there was no trickery, the King and all the court gathered round.

"Your Majesty," began Gaston, very slowly, "yesterday as I sat in the forest, the most beautiful princess in the world came to me and kissed me on the lips."

The Princess blushed.

"That is a clever lie," said the King, becoming uneasy, "but not nearly big enough to fill the sack."

"Your Majesty," Gaston began again, "yesterday a very wise king came to me, knelt down, and began to kiss—"

"That will do!" screamed the King. "The sack is more than filled!"

So Gaston the shepherd married the Princess, and when the King finally died, Gaston succeeded him.

JOHN SHEA AND THE FAIRY TREASURE

IRELAND

JOHN SHEA was a poor farmer who lived alone on a piece of scraggily land near the village of Banog in Munster. He had neither parents to love him nor a wife to care for him, and the overworked soil hardly yielded enough food to keep him alive, in spite of the long hours he toiled.

"To be sure," he thought one day, "I might as well be killed in a foreign land as die of starvation here." So he put on his best shirt and trousers and his cap and set his feet on the road to the city of Cork. Once there he made straight for the docks where he spoke to the captain of a schooner that was about to sail for Denmark and got a job on board.

When the schooner arrived in Denmark, John bade the captain goodbye and set out to see the country. As he was walking down a long and lovely road, sheltered on both sides by well-trimmed hedges, he saw in the distance a fine castle whose grounds were nothing but fields of shaggy weeds.

"Well," thought John, "perhaps I can earn some food there, being handy as I am with scythe and rake," and he made his way to the castle, swung open the great front door, and went in. When his eyes became accustomed to the darkness, he found himself in a long panelled room. At the far end sat two old men with long smoky beards falling to their waists; between them sat an old hag with hair that fell over her eyes.

"Don't stand there, boy!" bellowed one of the old men. "Come and show yourself and tell us why you have been so long in coming."

"I seek work," mumbled John, surprised by his welcome, "and your grounds could use the hand of a gardener."

The bearded men looked at each other and nodded, while the woman moaned, "Is it the man, is it the man?"

"Hush, sister!" said one of the old men before turning again to John, who stood twisting his cap in his hands. "Very well, boy, but you shall receive no pay until the grass is cut to our liking."

John set to work and did not stop till he had the weeds and grass cut and raked; till the yard was as trim as a bowling green, except for a black stone that he could not move. "Nay," he thought, "all the men in Munster could not lift that weight." And he sat down on the stone to rest.

As he mopped his brow, one of the little old men came out and offered to help move the stone. To John's amazement the old man had the strength of a youth, and the stone lifted quite easily.

Under the stone was a pot of silver pieces. The old man filled John's pockets so full that he was sure his suspenders would break.

"You look like the willing and honest lad we have been waiting for," said the old man. "My brother and I have decided to send you on a journey for us. Is it true that you come from Ireland?"

" 'Tis true—from Banog near Dingle," answered John proudly.

"Ah! Then you know Dingle well. Listen closely to what I have to tell you. You are to take a ship and go quickly back home. Buy a fine leg of mutton and a creel of turf to make a fire. Two fields from your farm you will find a fairy fort. Roast the mutton near the fairy fort, then hide yourself.

"As the smell of the roasting spreads across the fields, a black cat who is the guardian of the fairy fort will come out. When she sees the mutton she will eat it and fall asleep. Kill her quickly and throw her body into the burning turf. Then go into the fort, where you will find a basin, a towel, and a razor. Bring them to me as quickly as possible and be sure that you touch nothing else, for if you do an evil spell will fall on you and you will not escape. Go, then, and good luck!"

With that the little man disappeared into the darkness of the castle.

John Shea went back home to Banog near Dingle, and after he had greeted all his friends and bought them a treat with his silver, he went to the market. There he bought a leg of the finest mutton and a creel of turf as he had been instructed. He told not a soul of his intentions but went to the field that was two fields from his home, and sure enough he saw a fairy fort, and a very fine one it was too.

Everything happened exactly as the old man had said it would, and when John had killed the black cat he went straightway into the fort, and found the basin, the towel, and the razor. Then he spied a large barrel full of golden coins. His eyes grew large, and he thought "To be sure, with that gold I would never need to do a lick of work again." But the old man's warning rang in his ears, so he hastened away. Hiring a carriage, he went quickly to Cork and took a ship back to Denmark.

When John arrived at the castle the brothers and their sister were overjoyed to see him and prepared a great feast for him. But before he was allowed to eat, the elder of the brothers asked John to shave him.

"I cannot," said John, "for I have never shaved anyone in my life." (And this was indeed true, for he was too young to shave himself.)

But the old man insisted. So John set to work and, to his amazement, the old man changed to a youth of twenty. Next John shaved the second old man, who became a youth of eighteen. Then John combed the old hag's hair and, before his very eyes, she turned into a winsome lass of sixteen.

After the feast, John spent the night in a sound sleep. In the morning the two brothers came to him and handed him a loaded musket.

"Go into the fields and woods," they commanded, "and shoot the first animal you see. Then bring it to us."

John searched through the fields and forests, and the first animal he saw was a large field mouse. He shot it and took it back to the castle, where the brothers boiled it and cut it into four pieces. They each took a piece, and gave one to their sister and one to John.

As soon as John ate his portion he received the power to see all the places where gold was hidden, in Ireland and anywhere else.

"What are you going to do with this power we have given you?" the brothers asked him.

"Do?" gasped John Shea. "To be sure, I'll be the richest man in all Munster. I will put up a fine castle and have a

flock of people to work my land, and I shall never lift a spade again."

Then the brothers asked him to take a sip of the broth in which the mouse had been cooked. John did so, and the magic power left him as quickly as it had come.

"We are sorry," said the brothers, "but you are too greedy a man to have such riches, so you had best go back to your farm." Saying this, they thrust a few coins of silver into his hand to pay his passage home.

John Shea spent the rest of his life looking for fairy forts and places where gold was hidden. But he never found any. And when at last he died, he was still a very poor man.

FINLAY THE GIANT KILLER

SCOTLAND

LONG, long ago the Hebrides Islands off the coast of Scotland were over-run by giants. In time they were all killed or driven off by the courageous islanders, until only one family of giants remained. This family, which made its home in a long dark cave on a cliff that hung over the sea, was so rich, so cruel, and so crafty that the people of the Islands lived in terror lest the giants come to rob and destroy their homes.

Now there lived in the Islands a great hero and mighty hunter called Finlay the Changeling. He and his sister were the last of a family that had fought giants for hundreds of years.

Every day as Finlay left the house to go hunting with his dogs he would warn his sister, "Do not open the window to the north or let the fire go out." She always obeyed him and tended the hearth carefully; but one spring day she thought, "It is a lovely warm day! I will let the fire go out and open the windows to freshen the house."

In a little while she heard a soft knock. At the door stood a tall, handsome youth, dressed in fine clothes. He had two dogs at his heels and the reins of his steed in his hand.

"I was hunting and lost my way," he said. "Would so fair a lass give a drink of cold water to a stranger?"

The girl was completely captivated by her visitor (who was really the younger son of the giant family and had been skilfully disguised by his crafty mother). She invited him in and they talked long and attentively. When he rose to leave, he asked if he could return again the next day.

"But you must not tell your brother," said the young man, "for I fear he would forbid it. Tomorrow I will wait on the high hill to the north. When the windows are opened and no smoke comes from the chimney, I shall know that I am welcome."

After that he came every day, for as soon as Finlay left, his sister raked the coals from the hearth and threw open the windows.

At last the young man confessed who he was. But Finlay's sister was in love. "I do not care who you are," she said. "I will follow you anywhere."

"Your brother will never allow you to marry me," the giant replied. "But I love you so much I would kill him to have you. Let me tell you my plan."

That very day, as Finlay was coming home by the forest path, he happened upon a strange new dwelling.

"Good evening to you, Finlay Changeling," called a tiny gnarled old woman from the open door. She had an immense shawl on her head and was winding a tangled mass of wool into a ball.

"Good evening, Grandmother," said Finlay. "Who are you and how is it I have never seen your house before?"

"I am called the Wise-One," she answered, "and I have come to help you in your danger."

"I am the greatest hunter in the Islands, my dogs are the fleetest, my arrows the truest, and my sword the keenest. What danger could threaten me?"

"Your sister has fallen in love with the younger son of the

giants. This very night she plots with him to take your life. When you go home you will find a bed of new rushes laid for you. Beneath the rushes lies the giant, who will strangle you as you sleep.''

Finlay listened while the old woman told him what to do, then set off for home, promising to return the next day.

His sister greeted him gaily at the door. "The soup is boiling above the fire, brother, and I have laid a bed of new rushes for you. Tie the dogs tightly and come to the table."

Instead Finlay bade the dogs lie down in the corner, though they were growling and the hair was rising on their necks. "You are very thoughtful," he said to his sister. "Bring me a tub of cool water that I may wash my feet."

While the sister hastened to the well for a tub of water, Finlay carefully lifted the kettle of boiling soup from its hook. He threw the steaming liquid on the bed of new rushes, and the scalded giant leapt up with a shriek and ran screaming to the hills with his hands over his blinded eyes. Finlay's sister, seeing that she was undone, dropped the tub of water and, cursing her brother, ran after the giant.

Finlay's troubles had just begun. When the young giant reached home his family plotted revenge. His older brother wished to go himself but Laggan, the father of the giants, forbade it.

"A tricky enemy is Finlay the Changeling," said Laggan. "It will take wit to deal with him. I have five heads and they have kept me alive three hundred years. For the honour of the family I will go."

"Your five heads and my magic will work together,"

croaked his wife. "Enough talking. I will prepare you to avenge our son."

That night, as darkness lay over the Islands, Finlay sat alone before a roaring fire. His bow and sword were close at hand and his dogs lay restless at his feet. Neither the warmth of the fire nor the nearness of the dogs could dispel his foreboding.

"Fith, foth, there is a hinderance to hospitality in this house!" cried a voice suddenly. "The door is barred against the wandering stranger."

As Laggan began to tear the door from its hinges, Finlay seized his bow, climbed to the loft, and tore a hole in the thatched roof. Quickly he shot the eyes from two of the heads. Then he leapt down, sword in hand, as the door crashed in. The dogs attacked, and Finlay's sword swung quickly and deftly until the five heads were severed from the giant's shoulders.

In the morning Finlay twined the hair of the heads into a rope and went to see the Wise-One.

"Well done, valiant hand. I see the father of the giants will kill no more."

"It was my brave dogs who made it possible," Finlay replied.

"There is yet need of them," the Wise-One told him. "Tonight the elder son will come to avenge his father." And the old woman gave Finlay a handful of powder and told him what to do.

Finlay went home and spent the day digging a hole many feet deep in the centre of the cottage floor. Then he care-

fully laid thin boards over the hole. As night fell he waited with his dogs by the fire as before. Soon a rumbling like thunder sounded through the hills, boulder crashed against boulder, and tall trees snapped.

"Fi, foth, fugitive, the smell of an enemy is within these walls!" the giant shouted in the night, and the house trembled as he pushed the door in. Finlay cowered on the far side of the room, pretending to be badly frightened.

The giant stooped low to enter. Then with a crash his mighty form fell through the thin boards and he bellowed with rage.

Up leapt Finlay and threw the powder that the Wise-One had given him full in the giant's face. As the giant's huge hands rubbed his stinging eyes, the dogs seized his ears and hair and held him fast while Finlay slew him.

In the morning Finlay took the massive head to the Wise-One.

"Well done again, valiant hand, though your danger is greater than ever now. The great grey Cailleach, the mother of the giant clan, does not grieve for her family, for she has no tears. Instead her anger grows hotter and her hate is boundless. She is strong and her trickery is unmatched. Stay here awhile and gather strength, for she will seek you out at the tide's turning."

So Finlay rested all day and drank a strong tea of herbs that the Wise-One's daughter brewed for him.

Towards evening he returned home to prepare for the coming of the Cailleach. The night fell black and rain came with it. A tiny knock sounded at the door, so gentle that

Finlay scarcely heard it above the beating rain. The dogs growled deep in their throats. The knock came again, louder this time.

Sword in hand, Finlay opened the door. Before him stood a little bent old woman, not four feet high, wearing a dripping cape made of chicken feathers.

"Is it Finlay the slayer of giants who welcomes me this rainy night?"

"I am Finlay. Come in, old woman. Sit by the fire and dry yourself."

The old woman sat at one end of the bench and Finlay at the other. Soon the dogs became restless and began to growl.

"Tie up your dogs, Finlay my son. I fear they will bite me."

"I have no cord to tie them with, old woman."

"Take this," she said, unwinding a long piece of red thread from the iron-grey hair that fell over her stooped shoulders. Finlay took the thread and, pretending to tie up the dogs, made them lie together in a corner without moving.

"Are the dogs tied?" asked the old woman.

"There they are in the corner," answered Finlay. The old woman looked at the dogs and saw that they were lying close together, and she smiled to herself, believing that they were tied with her magic thread.

"I see you are growing bigger, old woman," said Finlay.

"It is just the feathers of my cape drying."

"Your teeth are getting longer, old woman," said Finlay.

With a wild shriek the Cailleach sprang up and sank her sharp front fang deep into Finlay's shoulder. A mighty struggle followed. They fought in the cottage until the walls crumbled. They fought in the yard until it was a quagmire. They fought on the stony ground until the rocks were crushed into sand.

At last the dogs seized hold of the feather cape and pulled it from the Cailleach. Without it her strength began to fail, and despite his wounds Finlay pinned her down, breaking her arm and her rib.

"You are the victor, Finlay. Let me go and I will never bother you again."

"There is no truth in your words, O Cailleach."

"I will give you a trunk of gold and a trunk of silver that are in my cave, Finlay."

"They are mine already, O Cailleach."

"I will give you a case of jewels that once belonged to fine lords and ladies."

"The jewels are mine already, O Cailleach."

"I will give you a gold-hilted sword that can overcome any man or beast on earth."

"The sword is mine already, O Cailleach."

"I will give you a magic wand," cried the old woman. "If you strike a stone pillar with it, the pillar will turn into a warrior. Strike the warrior again, and he will turn back into a pillar."

"The wand is mine already, O Cailleach."

The Cailleach was now very weak. Finlay let her go and the dogs tore her to pieces.

In the morning Finlay took the tattered feather cloak to the Wise-One.

"It is good to see you alive, valiant hand."

"I am alive and nothing more," replied Finlay.

"Rest here, and my daughter will heal your wounds with herbs and red moss," said the Wise-One.

Toward evening Finlay set out for the giants' cave with the Wise-One and her daughter. They gathered a load of heather and Finlay put it in the mouth of the cave. Just as the tide was coming in, he set fire to the heather and thick smoke filled the black cavern. Terrible were the curses and cries within the cave, and soon the blinded giant and Finlay's sister ran through the smoke and fell headlong into the sea. That was the last of the giants in all Scotland.

"The treasures are yours, Finlay," said the Wise-One. "But listen to me once more."

"Your advice has saved my life. I will accept it always."

"Take the trunk of gold and the trunk of silver for yourself, and return the case of jewels to the rightful owners. Anything that has magic in it cast into the sea."

"All this will I do, and gladly, O Wise-One."

Finlay became a hero to the people of the Islands. With his gold and silver and the Wise-One's daughter as his wife, he lived like a king for the rest of his days.

SWAN WHITE AND FOX-TAIL

SWEDEN

ONCE upon a time in the lovely land of Sweden, there lived a beautiful maiden whose name was Solveig. She was all alone in the world, for her parents were dead and her brother Sven had gone to make his fortune in a far land. Solveig was so poor that she was forced to live on the cold charity of an old woman who was a distant relative. Her only companion was the woman's daughter Gerd, a spiteful, disagreeable girl.

One fine spring morning, as Solveig was going to the village well for water, she plucked a sprig of blossoms from a thorn-apple tree and thrust it into the tattered shawl that covered her blond tresses. When she reached the well she paused for a moment to admire the blossoms in the clear water. Suddenly a small white hand shot up from the depths of the well.

"Give me the blossoms you have in your shawl," cried a thin voice. "I need them to brighten my world of shadows."

"Take them and welcome," said the girl gently as she put the fragrant spray into the hand. "Tell me, who are you? May I help you out of the well?"

"I am a water sprite, and this well has been my home for a hundred years," was the answer. "Should the sun shine on me I would disappear like the mist in the morning."

"Truly, I wish that I could help you," said Solveig.

"Such kindness is thrice blessed," the water sprite said. "I therefore give you threefold gifts. You shall be three times more beautiful. Your voice shall be three times more enchanting, so that when you laugh a golden ring shall fall from your lips. And wherever you walk three red roses shall grow from your footprints."

As Solveig was returning from the well she met the old woman and her daughter and told them that she had spoken with a water sprite. They laughed at her, but she accepted their mockery with her usual good nature and laughed herself. To her astonishment a small gold ring fell from her lips. She looked behind her and saw bouquets of red roses growing.

"I wasn't dreaming!" she cried. "The water sprite's gifts were real!"

From that time on Solveig was called Swan White, because of her graceful beauty. Everyone who knew her was happy for her good fortune except the women she lived with, and they nearly choked with envy.

"If Swan White can do it, so can I," said Gerd. She took a sprig from the thorn-apple tree and carried it to the well. As she held it over the water the same thin white hand reached up.

"Give me some blossoms to brighten my world of shadows," begged the voice of the water sprite.

"I am not one for giving presents," Gerd retorted. "There are certain wishes I want granted in return."

"I give you not wishes but curses," cried the sprite so angrily that steam rose from the water. "Henceforth you shall be three times as ugly. When you laugh, a black toad shall jump from your mouth. And wherever you tread, fox-tails shall grow in your steps."

Gerd spat in the water. "Take that for your silly curses!"

she screamed, and ran wildly home. But even as she ran a path of ugly fox-tails sprang up behind her. Children stopped playing when they saw her and ran screaming to their mothers. People soon forgot her real name and called her Fox Tail.

Meanwhile, in a far-away land Swan White's brother Sven had taken service with a powerful king. He was a good and faithful servant and soon King Valdemar put him in charge of the royal household.

The other servants became angry that a foreigner had found such favour with the King, and began to whisper that Sven worshipped an idol. Soon, as had been intended, King Valdemar heard the rumour and set a spy to watch his servant day and night.

"Your Majesty," said the spy, "I fear that it is as you have heard. Every night your servant kneels before a portrait in his room and talks to it."

The King had Sven brought before the high court of the land, and asked him what he had to say in his own defence.

"In my far-away home," said Sven, "I left a young sister. Each night I kneel before her portrait and ask God to take care of her."

King Valdemar was touched by the youth's words and sent for the portrait. He could not take his eyes from it, so fascinated was he by the maiden's beauty.

"The fastest ship in my fleet is at your service," said the King. "Take it to your own country and bring back your sister. If she is as beautiful as this portrait I will make her my queen."

When Sven arrived at his old home with a ship-load of treasures and beautiful clothes, there was great excitement in the household. He told Swan White of his adventures, and of King Valdemar's wish.

"How could I ever learn to be a queen?" said Swan White. "What have I done to deserve such an honour?" But she promised to go with her brother because she loved him.

Fox Tail and her mother pretended to be very happy for Swan White, but their hearts were black with jealousy. They begged Sven to take them along, and to please his sister he agreed, though it was against his will. Soon they were ready to depart, for Swan White had few belongings to take with her aside from a little dog.

The voyage passed quickly, so happy was Swan White to be with her brother once again. Then, just as they neared the end of the journey, a terrible storm arose, and the ship was in great danger. Sven climbed to the top of the mast to keep watch.

Suddenly he saw the lights of the harbour. "Prepare to go ashore," he called to his sister, "for I see the royal barge coming to meet us!"

The roar of the wind and the crash of the billows drowned his voice and Swan White could not hear it. "What did my brother say?" she asked Fox Tail.

"He said cast yourself into the sea or we will all be drowned," Fox Tail answered slyly.

Because Swan White loved her brother and feared for his life more than her own, she leapt into the wild sea, where she was claimed by a mermaid.

Fox Tail dressed herself in some of Swan White's clothes and put a veil over her face. When the barge came alongside, she and Sven were taken ashore. They were led to the palace and greeted with much ceremony.

"Dear maiden," said the King to Fox Tail, "I have longed to see your beauty. Do me the honour of removing your veil."

Fox Tail threw back the veil, and grinning hideously, closed her eyes for a kiss.

King Valdemar's anger filled the palace.

"You have tricked me!" he shouted to Sven. "Your sister is the ugliest woman I've ever seen!" Calling his guards, he said, "Throw this fool to the lions! And send this ugly woman home."

In the mermaid's world beneath the sea Swan White was very unhappy. She begged to go and say goodbye to her brother and the little dog that she had brought with her on the journey. The mermaid was filled with pity that one so beautiful and so modest should be lost on the eve of great happiness. Though it was against the rules of the undersea world, she agreed to allow Swan White to go ashore twice, but not as a mortal. The mermaid turned her into a little white duck and put an invisible gold chain around her neck.

"Now be off with you," said the mermaid, "and come back as soon as I pull on the chain."

As Swan White was approaching the castle, she heard her dog barking mournfully. The sound led her to the kitchen of the palace where the animal had been given food and refuge.

"My little pet, I've found you!" Swan White whispered

to the dog, and kissed the animal on his wet nose.

All too soon Swan White felt the tug of the chain. Sadly she made her way back to the sea, leaving a path of red roses behind her. The servants gazed in wonder at the flowers, and one of the cooks picked an armful to decorate the table of the King.

"What marvelous roses these are!" said King Valdemar at dinner. "It is not the season for roses—where did you find them?"

The cook told him about the small white duck that had played with the stray dog.

The next day the King waited in the kitchen, and sure enough, just at suppertime, in came a little white duck, and the dog barked happily. After a few moments the duck and the dog bade each other farewell, for the mermaid had begun to pull the invisible chain.

As the duck turned to leave, King Valdemar seized it by one leg. The mermaid pulled the chain harder and harder, but the King held on tightly. The duck took the form of a slippery dragon that hissed and snarled. The King held on with all his might. Then the dragon changed into a fierce wolf, but still the King held on.

Suddenly the chain broke. At once Swan White became herself again.

"You are the maiden in the portrait!" cried King Valdemar, "but you are even lovelier than I thought. I beg of you, marry me without delay."

"I shall marry you and gladly," answered Swan White. "But where is my brother?"

The King paled. With his servants at his heels he ran to the lion pits. There he found Sven fast asleep, his pillow the largest lion of all!

The wedding that followed was a great occasion in the land, but greater still was the happiness that Swan White brought to her husband and his people.

OLLI AND THE RICH TROLL

FINLAND

ONCE upon a time in the south of Finland, on the side of a mountain sloping down to a bay, there lived a simple farmer. On the other side of the bay lived a wicked troll with his wife and three daughters.

One evening when all the chores were done, the farmer and his three sons were sitting on the porch. The old man pointed to the light in the troll's window across the bay and said, "It is strange, my boys! Here we are, honest men who labour hard for our living, but at the year's end we are as poor as when we started. Over yonder the wicked troll lives idly on, never getting old. He does no good in the world, yet he grows richer and richer."

Olli, the farmer's youngest son, said, "Father, I shall kill the troll and divide his treasures among the people from whom he steals."

But his two older brothers, Toivo and Tauno, laughed at him. "We will go and destroy the troll, and if you are brave enough, you are welcome to come and watch."

The next day the three brothers rowed across the bay and climbed the mountain to the troll's house. The troll very courteously invited them in and made them most welcome.

"Stay and eat with us," he said, and the brothers accepted.

When they sat down at the table for dinner, Toivo and Tauno ate a great deal and drank a lot of wine, but Olli only nibbled at his food and took no wine, saying he was too young.

After the meal the troll said to the youths, "Young men,

you look like honest fellows and good providers. If you agree to marry my daughters, I promise to divide my fortune among you." And he showed them his money-bag, which he kept under his pillow.

The troll's daughters were quite pretty, and Toivo and Tauno agreed at once. After all, they reasoned, why go to the trouble of killing the troll when they could gain his treasure with so little effort?

It was growing very dark and the bay was too rough for a boat. The troll bade the boys stay for the night, and put down more sleeping mats; his wife put white night-caps on the three boys and red night-caps on the three girls. Then they both went outside.

Toivo and Tauno suspected nothing and were soon fast asleep. But Olli was cautious. He remained awake until all the others were snoring. Then he quietly switched the night-caps about, putting the red caps on himself and his brothers and the white caps on the sleeping troll girls.

Shortly afterwards the wicked old troll entered with a long knife and cut off the three heads with the white caps. He left the room chuckling, and saying, "What a feast we shall have tomorrow, for they are all so young and tender."

When the troll had gone, Olli wakened his brothers. Together they crept quietly into the barn and took the troll's horse, a beautiful creature with a mane of gold and a coat of silver. Then they sped away.

Some time later Olli begged his brothers to go back with him to steal the troll's money-bag, but they were afraid.

"Then I shall go alone," said Olli.

When he arrived, he was greeted at the door by the old troll-wife. "My husband is not home, Olli," she croaked, "but you are welcome. Wait until my bread is baked and eat some with me."

Olli told her to rest, that he would watch the bread for her. As soon as she closed her eyes, Olli put more fuel on the fire and opened the damper; the bread began to burn, and smoke filled the room. The old woman jumped up, and as she scrambled to save the loaves, Olli seized the money-bag and ran off.

When the troll came home, he walked down to the foot of the mountain and shouted across the bay, "Olli, was it you who stole my money-bag?"

"Yes," answered Olli, "but it is *my* money-bag now."

Some time later Olli decided to visit the troll's house once more, for he wanted a golden coverlet that he had seen there. This time he left at night, carrying a drill, a saw, a fishing-line with a hook on it, and a bottle of water.

When he reached the troll's house he climbed to the roof and bored several holes; then he poured the water through the holes, wetting the golden coverlet. The sleepy troll-wife, noticing the dampness, picked up the coverlet and hung it in the rafters to dry.

Olli now cut a small hole in the roof with his saw, dropped the fishing-line through it, snagged the coverlet, and drew it up. Then he climbed down and sped off with his golden catch.

The next day the troll shouted across the bay, "Olli, was it you who stole my golden coverlet?"

"Yes," answered Olli, "but it is *my* coverlet now."

A little while later Olli told his father that there was yet another thing he wanted from the troll's house—a little golden bell that sat on a table near the door. Taking his saw, he set out at night as he had done before. When he was sure the troll and his wife were asleep, he cut a small hole in the wall, and reached in. But as he groped for the bell, he knocked it to the floor. The troll awoke, leapt up, and seized Olli's arm. Then the troll-wife ran outside, slipped a fishnet over Olli's head, and held him fast while the troll bound him hand and foot.

"Heat the oven at once," the troll ordered his wife, "while I go and invite the other troll-people to join us for a feast this very night!"

When the old woman had the oven nice and hot, she opened the oven-door wide, unbound Olli, and told him to get inside. But Olli pretended not to understand what she meant and asked her to show him. When the old woman bent over and stuck her head in the oven door, Olli gave her a hard kick, pushing her in completely. He found some straw and covered it with blankets on the troll-wife's bed so that it looked as if she was fast asleep. Then he put the golden bell inside his shirt and went home.

Just before dawn the wicked troll came home with a great crowd of his troll friends, all hungry and eager for the feast. He peeped into the bedroom, saw what he thought was his wife's sleeping form, and let her be. Now he and his friends would have more to eat.

How they feasted!

Suddenly the troll's knife struck something hard and he drew out some beads.

"My wife's necklace!" he cried. "That Olli has tricked me again!" He rushed to the bed and found the straw. Then he ran down to the bay and called out across the water, "Olli, did you roast my old woman?"

"Your old woman?" cried Olli. "Is she not behind you?"

The troll turned quickly and was blinded by the sun just rising over the mountain top. Before he could blink he burst, for a troll can never look at the sun.

Olli and his brothers then collected all the valuables in the troll's house and in his secret cellars and divided them among their neighbours, keeping only enough to buy farms for themselves.

As for the other trolls, they fled from the terrible Olli, and since then no troll has dared to live in Southern Finland.

THE KING'S THIEF

GERMANY

LONG, long ago, when the country that is now Germany was a land of forests and fields and small kingdoms, there lived in the smallest kingdom of all a thief who was so clever that he had never been caught, and so successful that he was reputed to be as rich as the King.

Wherever people met they talked of the clever thief. Even the King's courtiers spoke of little else, until the King grew weary of the chatter.

"Robbing fools is easy," he said. "This thief could never rob me!"

When the thief heard what the King had said, his pride was stung. He sent a message to the King begging to be allowed to demonstrate his art for one week without fear of arrest.

His request was granted. The next day he arrived at the palace and was presented to the King.

"Do you see that ploughman working my field?" said the King, pointing out the window. "I dare you to steal the oxen from under his nose."

The thief looked at the sky; though the sun was shining, he saw a black cloud looming up. He looked carefully at the the field and saw that it was bordered on one side by dense woods. Without a word he bowed to the King and slipped away.

Off he went into the woods and began to whistle and chirp like a flock of frightened birds. The peasant, hearing the noise, looked up and saw the black cloud coming. Certain that a shower would soon be upon him, he left his plough in the furrow and ran to the shelter of the trees. Quick as a flash, the thief unyoked the oxen and drove them off.

"It is easy enough to steal oxen from a ploughman," said the King when the thief returned. "But I defy you to steal my black charger from the royal stables."

The thief smiled faintly, bowed again, and left.

That night the King tripled the guard at the stables. "There is a clever thief in the palace," he told the captain of the guard. "If my horse is not here in the morning, you will all be punished!"

When everyone had retired for the night the thief stole the uniform of the Master of the Royal Bedchamber and put it on. Taking a barrel of wine from the cellars, he carried it carefully to the stables. When he was challenged by the captain of the guard, he whispered, "Stand down, good man. The thief has been captured and is to be hanged in the morning. His Majesty bids you celebrate, and as a reward for your diligence sends you this wine. But you must not sing or you will disturb His Majesty's rest."

The guards were happy to obey. Soon the barrel was almost empty, and one by one the men dropped into the straw and fell asleep. Quick as a flash the thief mounted the unguarded horse and galloped away.

As soon as the sun had risen, the King strode to the stable, where he found his charger gone and the guards lying about snoring. He kicked the captain awake, and the captain kicked the sergeant, and the sergeant kicked the corporal,

and the corporal kicked the men. As they all stood about with straw in their hair looking foolish, the captain tried to explain. "But, but . . . Your Majesty, your chamberlain told us —"

"That was not the chamberlain!" screeched the King. "That was the thief!"

Later that morning, in the throne room of the palace, the thief bowed low before the King and said, "I have returned the black charger, Your Majesty."

"You are a clever man," said the King begrudgingly, "but there is something I *know* you cannot steal—the diamond ring the Queen wears upon her finger."

That evening there was a palace dinner, and everyone was so busy flying back and forth from the kitchen to the great banquet room that no one noticed an extra servant. Dressed as a butler, the thief carefully observed the arrangement of the palace rooms. He even found his way to the royal bed-chamber and saw where the one high window was.

After his guests had gone home the King quadrupled the guard around the palace and provided the men with fierce dogs on long chains. Then he made a tour of inspection, warning each soldier in turn. He did not notice that he was being followed by a man in a captain's uniform who gave each dog a bone covered with glue. As the dogs began to chew the bones their jaws became stuck and they could not bark.

When this man approached the guard who was stationed beneath the King's window, he whispered, "As soon as the light goes out in the royal chamber, set a ladder carefully against the wall, for I have heard that the thief is hidden in the palace and will probably leap from that very window."

The sleepy guard saluted and promised to obey.

The King blew out the candle and tumbled into bed. "That rascal will never find his way in here tonight!" he said happily. But before his eyes were closed he heard a scraping sound on the wall outside. He leaned out the window, saw the ladder against the wall, and rushed downstairs.

The thief, who had been hiding in an ante-room, quickly entered the bedchamber and in the King's voice said, "Well, we caught the thief as he was climbing a ladder to the window. But he might escape, so give me the ring and I will lock it in the strong-box for the night."

"Here it is," murmured the Queen sleepily as she held out the beautiful diamond that glittered in the moonlight. The thief took it and left the room.

A few moments later the King returned. "That is the end of the rascal," he said. "My guards caught him as he was placing a ladder beneath this window."

"I know," answered the Queen without fully waking. "You told me all that five minutes ago, when you took the ring."

The King gasped. "Took the ring!" he screamed. "I didn't take the ring!" And he knew that he had been tricked once more.

In the morning the thief appeared before the King.

"Your Majesty," he said, and bowed. "I have found a ring so rare that it belongs only on a queen's hand. Take it as a gift to honour me!"

Not wishing to let so crafty a man out of his sight, the King made the thief finance minister and a duke as well. Never again did any of the King's subjects grumble about their taxes, for the clever thief took their money with so much skill that they scarcely knew it was gone.